Olive's Birthday

*by **Elizabeth Milbourn***

Published by Clink Street Publishing 2022

Copyright © 2022

First edition.

ISBN:

978-1-914498-21-3 - paperback
978-1-914498-22-0 - ebook

1

Olive **leapt** out of bed and ran into her mummy and daddy's room.

"It's my birthday!" she **shouted**.

"Huh...?" mummy and daddy mumbled, sitting **up** in bed.

Olive **jumped** on the bed and gave her parents a **jiggle**.

"Happy birthday Olive!" they said.

3

Present Time!

"There are **three** presents hidden in your room," said daddy. "See if you can find them."

Which present did Olive find first?

Choose a page...

Go to page **6**

or

Go to page **8**

or

Go to page **10**

4

Happy birthday
Olive x

5

Olive found a **blue** present **under** her bed.

Go to page **12**

A soft, furry **tiger** costume.

"My **favourite** animal!"
Olive squealed.

7

Olive found an orange present
behind her orangutan.

Glow in the dark pyjamas.

'Let's try them out!"
shouted Olive.

Go to
page 12

Happy birthday
Olive x

Olive found a **purple** present **under** her pillow.

Go to next page

Huh, a **potato**?

"That's a **weird** present,"
Olive muttered.

11

Party Time!

After some **more** presents, Olive had a **yummy** pancake birthday breakfast. Before long it was time to get **dressed** for her **party**.

What sort of party was Olive having?

Choose a page...

Go to page **14**

or

Go to page **16**

or

Go to page **18**

12

An adventure park party!

Olive and her friends got to hold a tortoise and a *slithery* snake.

Then they went pond **dipping**.

Then they rode *go*-karts.

Go to page 20

A **tidying up** party! Urgh.

Actually, the party was **lots** of fun. Olive and her friends **noisily** tossed tin cans *into* bins.

Then they *raced* each other in **sack** races.

Then they made junk **model** robots and the **best** robot won a prize.

1st PRIZE

Go to page **20**

A bouncy castle party!

Olive and her friends **bounced** and **bounced**.

Then they played **pass-*the*-parcel**.

Go to next page

Then they played **musical** statues.

HAPPY BIRTHDAY

Dad's famous potato salad

19

Cake Time!

After having some **party** food,
it was **time for cake**.

What sort of cake did
Olive have?

Choose a page...

Go to page **22**

or

Go to page **24**

or

Go to page **26**

Ew! A *slimy* slug cake! Look at those g^oogly eyes.

Everyone sang **Happy Birthday**, and when
Olive *blew* out her candles, she made a wish.

What would **you** wish for?

Actually, the cake was **delicious**.
It was *vanilla sponge* with chocolate icing.

Go to page **28**

The *slime* was really **jelly** and
the g^oogly eyes were sweets.

Wow! A pirate ship cake!

Look at all that **treasure.**

Everyone sang *Happy Birthday*, and when Olive *blew* out her candles, she made a **wish.**

Go to page **28**

What would **you** wish for?

Wow! A superhero cake!

Look at that costume.

Everyone sang *Happy Birthday*, and when Olive *blew* out her candles, she made a wish.

Go to next page

What would YOU wish for?

At the **end** of the **party**, Olive handed out party bags.

"That was the best birthday E...E...**EVER.**" she said, yawning loudly.

When mummy and daddy tucked Olive into bed that night Olive asked, "How many sleeps until my *next* birthday...?!"

Lightning Source UK Ltd.
Milton Keynes UK
UKHW051213140322
400022UK00005B/60